CHAINED UP AT THE HUCOW PRISON

Steamy Milking Story

Leandra Camilli

ISBN: 9798836597221
Imprint: Independently published

1st edition

Cover design by: Leandra Camilli

CONTENTS

CHAPTER 1

"There was someone I knew that was in your position," the lawyer said, looking at me with concerned eyes, even though, checking out his face, I knew that he was feeling no pity for me.

It was like he was trying to convince me to do something, but I had no idea what that was.

I was in his office and he was sitting across the desk, looking at me as he reclined in his chair. He was absolutely stunning. One of the most handsome men I had seen in my life.

One of the things I first noticed about him when I stepped inside his office was that he was so much taller than me. I could see that my eyes were level with his nipples, which was something that didn't happen often.

Most of the men I knew weren't that tall, where I lived. I could just imagine myself in his arms, feeling the heat of his body, the beating of his heart, his fingers dancing on my skin, feeling it, and then his hot lips crashing down on mine.

Just thinking about that happening was already hardening my nipples, which was, in turn, making me blush. Dammit! I had no idea what was going on with me, but this was concerning on all levels.

Charles was most likely looking at me and wondering what I was thinking. I looked so innocent, too, even though I was anything but. I couldn't help myself. My hands were clasped between my thighs and I was trying to make myself as small as possible, even though that wasn't working well.

After all, if there was something that people always told me I was, it was that I was curvy and busty. And yes, I pretty much was. Those were some of the few things about me I was proud of and that I always rubbed in the faces of the people I didn't like.

Usually, those were my enemies. Girls from my former high school class that thought I was less than them. But then I proved I wasn't, and now here I was, talking to my lawyer, who was most likely going to give me two options - either go to a normal prison or the Hucow Prison, and thinking about the latter... I couldn't help but feel extreme levels of anxiety.

I just never thought that this would happen. I thought that nobody would find out about what I did to my enemies. Those bitches... I hated them so much I just wanted to see them dead.

That wasn't what I did, though. It was something much less drastic.

"Ms. Cisneros?" Charles asked, his head behind his hands and his elbows on the desk, looking at me as though he was thinking about asking another question, but he was going to weigh his words better this time. After all, this was more difficult for him than it was for me. "You need to think about your choices and what you can do."

And with that said, I perked my head up. "Take me to a normal prison. I don't think I want to go to the Hucow Prison."

And having said that, he took a deep breath and then stood up and went around the desk. My heart started to beat faster than normal, and I could feel sweat coming out of the pores of my skin. He was going to go behind me, wasn't he?

It was an idiotic question. I knew he was going to do that, thus it wasn't surprising when I felt him putting his hands on my shoulders. The audacity of this man! And yet, something about the way that his fingers were pressing against my skin sent cracks of electricity through my body.

My pussy was beginning to get wet and I couldn't do anything about that. I was just hoping that his nose wasn't perceptive enough. If that wasn't the case, then for sure he was going to notice the smell of my arousal.

"I think I can change your mind about that," he murmured behind me and even though his face was far from my head, I still felt his hot breath swirling around my neck, sending ripples of arousal down my spine.

"What do you mean? I just don't want to be subjected to a place where they are going to milk me and change me so much that I would be unrecognizable."

I could hear him sniffing and I knew he was smelling my arousal. Realizing that made me feel even more concerned than I was, and I started to rub my legs together, doing everything in my power to contain my increasing arousal.

But it was all pointless. I was getting hornier and hornier by the second, and Charles was using that to his advantage.

"If you decide to go to a common prison, your sentence won't be lowered, you won't be able to see anyone you want, you won't get any money for anything you do there, and you will also live there for so long that you will come out of there completely unrecognizable. I know it's up to you, but I think that the best option for you is pretty clear. Spend a couple of years in the Hucow Prison, get milked a couple times, and then come out of there looking like a heroine that doesn't owe the world anything."

I wasn't going to deny that it was tempting, but I couldn't even think about that properly when he was with his nose almost rubbing on the back of my neck.

Then, he moved away and sat back down in his chair. He clasped his hands together on the desk and then gazed at me with questioning eyes.

"So, have I managed to change your mind?" He asked and I finally had enough space and time to think about it more clearly. Then, I closed my eyes, thought about it a little more, and decided to choose my words carefully so that I didn't make a huge mistake.

"All right, I'm changing my mind and I'm going to the Hucow Prison, but I hope that I'm not making a mistake."

He opened a wicked smile.

"You aren't."

CHAPTER 2

The Hucow Prison was one of the most fearsome places I had seen in my life. Just standing in front of it was making me feel shivers down my spine. There was this police officer that was behind me and he was pushing his gun on my back, making me follow the line with other candidates that were going to become hucows as well.

He was quite impatient, grumbling, "Hurry up. I don't know what you think this is, but it certainly isn't your next vacation."

I looked behind my shoulder, narrowing my eyes slightly. I was hoping that it was going to make him think twice about talking to me that way and using that tone, but he just shrugged his shoulders, pushing his assault rifle against my back again.

The metal was cold and unfriendly.

Checking him out from bottom to top, there was no denying that he was also a stunning man. Not as tall as Charles, my lawyer, but he was still at the top of the list of towering men.

His face sported a full, perfect beard. His hair was short and pitch-black and painted with some streaks of gray. His eyes, ocean blue, showed his attention and that he was focused on just one thing right now – finishing today's shift, going back home, collapsing onto his couch, and then watch tonight's football game.

He looked like a Greek god, and I couldn't help but imagine what it would be like to slither my fingers over his muscles, feeling their hardness and how firm they were.

Checking his face a little more again, I could see that he was much older than me. Probably by a decade at least, but even though that was something that made me feel some wetness in my pussy, it was nothing more than a detail. An exciting detail, but still nothing more than that.

He got a haircut recently and it suited him well. It also made him look even more appetizing than he was, instigating me to want to thread my fingers through his hair after he kissed me for what felt like an eternity.

Even though he wore a police uniform, I could see the way his muscles strained against the material, almost making me fear they were going to rip it into pieces.

Unfortunately, that didn't happen.

The line moved forward and I had to follow it. I turned my head back around so that I was focusing on it and not on the massive man walking behind me, still with his assault rifle pressing against my back.

After a moment of silence, I could feel his eyes assessing every part of me. If that was the case, I wouldn't be able to stop myself from feeling even more aroused than I was right now. After all, I was pretty sure that he was either married or had a girlfriend, in which case he would never even have eyes for me - not even if he wanted to explore a little bit beyond his relationship.

Then, we were finally inside the prison and Patrick marched off somewhere. I checked him as he went into another room in the prison, and I couldn't help but wonder where he was going.

After all, during the whole time that he was guiding me inside the prison, I was certain that he was checking my behind. And he had every reason to be doing that, considering the kind of man he was – or probably was, I corrected myself, not wanting to draw any conclusions before I knew more about him.

I was naked. When we came to the prison, everyone was. It was one of the requirements. The transformation was going to begin shortly and since our bodies were going to change so much, we couldn't be wearing clothes.

Where I lived, I was used to being naked pretty much all the time. It was one of the things that my enemies started to pick on when they were studying with me. They thought I had dementia or something like that, but I never gave that much attention.

We were in this massive, sprawling entrance hall when I felt someone grabbing my hand. It was the hand of a woman, I immediately noticed when I felt how soft and smooth it was. It was also remarkably small.

I looked down and I found someone that had already gone through the transformation. It was another woman that looked similar to me, but she was much bigger – and that was something I didn't usually say often about anyone.

She was gazing at me with dreamy eyes, as though she could see everything that happened to her happen to me as well. I had no idea if that was likely, but I wasn't thinking about it much.

What I was thinking about was what she had to tell me.

"You are new here, aren't you?"

I nodded. "I am. What's your name?"

"It's Mary. Mary Hurt. I'm so glad that it looks like you are enjoying your time here, especially given that you've just arrived."

I checked my surroundings again, turning my head left and right. "It really is a scary place, though, don't you think?"

"I don't think it's scary," she replied, moving her hands around her massive belly, which showed that she was pregnant. "I think that it's the perfect place for you. I'm sure you're going to find your bull in here."

"My bull?" I asked, not knowing why she used that term, though I had a suspicion that could explain her behavior. I knew that I was going to become a hucow just like she was, but I never thought that the men were called bulls.

"Your mate. The one that is going to get you pregnant so that you can make more and better milk."

I curled up one of my eyebrows, finding that weird. Someone here knocked me up so that I could make better and more milk?

It was just weird, but also remarkably lust-inducing, and thus it wasn't long until I started to ask Mary more questions about what she had just mentioned.

I was curious and I knew that I had to know as much as I could before the transformation.

CHAPTER 3

I was on the operation table and they were going to start my transformation. The doctors surrounded me. They were walking around me, talking to me, reassuring me, and trying to make this as less painful as possible. But it was still unnerving, especially because they walked everywhere as if this was one of the most complicated operations of their lives.

But it couldn't be. This was just like any other operation, right?

I moved my finger up, catching the attention of one of the doctors. He was one of the doctors that hadn't been talking to me since I entered the operation room, and something about his face showed me that he was someone I knew.

Or at least, I thought he was someone I knew.

It took me a couple seconds, but I eventually realized that I was right about that. He was none other than Charles, my lawyer, and I couldn't help but wonder why he was here and was pretending to be a doctor.

He looked the part. A white gown, gloves, a mask, that little cap on his head, and the look in his eyes that showed me how confident he was about this.

It was actually the only thing that was making me less nervous about this, remembering that I was naked and he could see every part of me now.

"What are you doing here, Charles?" I asked, feeling some wetness in my pussy.

"I came here to see you. After we talked in my office, I was so curious about your operation and how it was going to turn out.

I was so curious about seeing how you were going to look when your transformation finished."

And then, he pressed his finger against my pussy, sliding it up and making me feel cracks of electricity traveling in my body.

I didn't know how good it was to be felt like that, his fingers still pressing against my pussy lips as if he was entitled to do that, and considering the confident look in his eyes, I could tell that he was indeed thinking he was.

"Really? I thought I was no one to you."

"You should give more credit to yourself," he said, dipping his finger in my pussy and then starting to move it back and forth, instigating ripples of pleasure in my body. "You are, actually, one of the most stunning women I've seen in my life."

I widened my eyes. I never thought someone would ever say something like that to me, and much less that that person was going to be none other than Charles.

He took his finger out of my cunt and I couldn't help but press my legs against his arm, stopping him from doing what I considered to be a sin.

"Please don't stop doing that. It's the only thing that's actually making me feel less nervous about this."

He slid his other hand along my arm, feeling my skin and comforting me.

"Actually, this is just for show – for the most part. Your transformation happens with an injection." And after he said that, he produced a syringe, showing it to me clearly.

"Really? And here I was so worried about this," I said before he injected into me the substance that was in the syringe. It was clear and cold, and I felt it running in my veins.

Then, I felt his fingers playing with my mound, enjoying it, instigating more ripples of pleasure in my body. I couldn't help but move my legs slightly apart so that I wasn't locking his arm anymore.

Seconds later, he finally had enough space to move his arm away. I thought he was going to do that, especially because I was already anything but my usual self.

His fingers brushing and dancing on my snatch was making me feel so wet, my nipples so hard, I thought I was going to come. And Charles, even though he was well aware of that, didn't stop his assault. If anything, he kept on doing what he was, his fingers now torturing my clit.

The waves of lust and pleasure that were traveling in my body were so overwhelming I couldn't hold it back any longer. Seconds later, my body started to writhe, convulse, and shake uncontrollably. I was coming so hard I knew I was most likely going to pass out and even though the straps could barely hold me to the table, Charles continued to do what he was doing, his fingers dipping inside my cunt one more time.

This time, he wasn't moving his hand anywhere else. He kept his fingers inside my snatch, rubbing, turning them, and putting them as deep inside me as he could.

Seconds after that, my body finally started to calm down after my relentless climax. I could barely hold it together, and I couldn't stop my eyes from closing.

Then, as if he intended to continue to torment me by doing this, Charles took his fingers out of my cunt and then moved so that he was right by the side of my head. I felt him putting his hand on my forehead, brushing his fingers on it slowly and gently.

"Don't worry. When you wake up, your transformation will be finished and you'll be so much more than who you are right now."

And I couldn't help but wonder if that meant he was going to be the first one to milk me.

CHAPTER 4

When I woke up, I realized I wasn't in the operation room anymore. Actually, I was somewhere completely different. I was chained up to the wall behind me, opening my eyes and realizing that something was odd and sticking out about this.

There was this huge mirror standing in front of me and it showed me. I couldn't help but widen my eyes, seeing my new self and noticing how much different I looked now.

I couldn't help but wonder if it would even be possible to walk normally and without difficulty now that my body was so heavy. I decided not to think too much about that and focused on my hanging, massive boobs, my ass, and my clit, which was raging and harder than it had ever been.

In the meantime, I also checked every part of this room that I could see, which looked more like a basement of sorts.

A man was with me and he was none other than Patrick Olden, the same police officer that was dabbing the mouth of his assault rifle on me while making me follow the line that I actually wanted to follow. After all, after deciding to come to the Hucow Prison, I didn't want to go anywhere, and that was telling. He should have known that just by looking at me.

But now... I could tell that he couldn't care less about that and was just using this opportunity to show off. What else would I be thinking right now, after all, especially after seeing the massive boner that he was sporting? It was even making me think that, perhaps, he was bigger and thicker than Charles, and that was saying something – I never even thought I would be thinking something like that.

He took a step forward until he was under the light hanging from the ceiling. His eyes sized me up, and then he took a couple more steps in my direction, eventually finding himself so close to me that I knew he could smell my arousal.

And, it wasn't surprising when he started to massage my mound after looking into my eyes and reading what I was thinking. It was impossible to say no to him, especially after seeing him moving his tongue across his lips, showing me how much he was enjoying every moment of this.

"You're absolutely stunning, and I can't help but wonder what your milk tastes like," he murmured, putting his other hand under my boob and pressing his fingers into it, shooting ripples of pleasure in my body. I knew he was good at this and was going to do something I found pleasing, but I didn't think that it was this good, and especially that his fingers were so warm.

As he pressed his fingers into my boob, a line of my milk came out, spreading over his hand. He lifted it, moving his fingers toward his mouth, and then licked them clean one by one right in front of me.

I should be feeling pissed off that he did that, but I was actually feeling the opposite. It was actually turning me on, my wetness building up in my pussy.

"Jesus, it's so fucking tasty," he murmured, moving his fingers toward my mouth, and I thought he was going to make me taste my own milk.

But that was disgusting and if there was milk I wanted to taste right now, it was his.

That was why I shook my head and said, "I don't want to taste my milk. I want to taste your milk, Daddy."

And as I said that last word, he blinked once and quickly, showing me that he didn't expect me to say it.

"You are already calling me your 'Daddy'?" He murmured, putting his other hand on my boob and then pressing it, making lines of my milk squirt out and hit his uniform. He still wore his police uniform, and it only made this hotter and more arousing.

One of my dreams was to be fucked by a police officer, and it was happening right at this moment.

"So much more milk," he murmured, putting his mouth where the milk was coming out of, opening it, and then drinking as much of it as he could.

This was messy, my milk coming out in lines that hit his face and lips and also even the top side of his torso.

I knew that my milk was delicious, but I didn't think that he was going to be so addicted to it that he was almost drinking everything I had. And I wasn't saying something that didn't make sense. It was the opposite of that, actually.

My jugs were getting empty, and as time continued to pass and the police officer continued to milk me, that was only becoming more evident.

Then, he looked up after moving his tongue across his lips again, licking as much of my milk as he could.

"Are you sure that you don't want it?" He insisted, sliding his hand gently over my shoulders until he finally cupped my neck. I didn't think he was going to start choking me, but it was a possibility, and with me chained up to the wall like this, he could do that with little effort. I wouldn't be able to struggle against him or do anything else to stop him.

I shook my head, confirming what I said before, "I'm not. I can't. I want your milk and I want you to knock me up."

I never thought I would one day be saying something like that to a man, but it was happening and it just felt right.

"Whatever you wish, but you should know that I'm not the only one who has been thinking about you a lot recently," he murmured, and as soon as he finished saying that, I heard footsteps coming down the stairs that led to this basement.

And they were familiar footsteps. It was Charles, and he was coming to milk me, too.

CHAPTER 5

The last thing I thought I was going to see – or rather someone – was Charles. I thought that this was something happening only between me and Patrick and that he wasn't involved in it as well.

That was why I was so surprised, my eyes so wide that I probably looked stupid.

"Adrienne, it's good to see you one more time," he murmured, already removing his clothes and finally revealing, to the delight of my eyes, how perfect his body was. Rippling muscles, a large and impressive tattoo of an eagle on his chest, and abs that made me feel like moving my hands all over them for as long as I could.

Then, he stood in front of me and started to lower me, even while I was still chained to the wall, so that my mouth was level with his cock. It was big, so much so I doubted I could fit it in my mouth, but of course I didn't say that to him. The last thing I wanted to do right now was anything that could piss him off.

My mouth watered. I never thought I would be face to face with a dick so big. I couldn't help but look up, wondering if I had his permission. Then, he nodded and I knew that I had what I was looking for.

I was going to be able to suck him off, and this was going to happen exactly like Mary told me it was. I was going to suck him off and then he was going to penetrate me with his slab of meat, and then he was going to knock me up, putting his baby in my belly, and that thought alone was already making my pussy so moist right now.

I couldn't waste any time, already diving my head, my lips wrapping around his prick and bobbing up and down on it eagerly. It was messy from the get-go, and more often than not his cock would slip out of my mouth, only then to be shoved back inside at the next moment.

I also didn't hold anything back as I started to monopolize and worship his balls, which were as big and heavy with his milk as I thought. As that happened, Charles took position behind me, his hands feeling and cherishing my skin, enjoying how smooth and soft it was.

I could also feel his hot breath against my neck, and it was as exciting and lust-inducing as I thought it was. Then, he slid his hand down my back, eventually finding my ass and fumbling with it before finally reaching my asshole.

And as he started to prod and play with it, he took his clothes off in a heartbeat, almost ripping them. In less than a couple of seconds, he was naked from top to bottom, and I had the opportunity to glance over my shoulder, catching a glimpse of it.

He was also built like a god, but his body was cleaner and he didn't have any tattoos on it – none that I could see, at least. He could have a tattoo on his back and I just couldn't see it right now.

"Gosh, you are so delicious," he purred, sliding his prick into my asshole, one inch at a time, starting to piston in and out of me slowly in the beginning. Then, he quickly picked up the pace and started to slap his hips against my ass so angrily and fast I thought he was going to come right at this moment.

But he didn't, making me surprised by the fact that he was fucking me so raw I thought he was going to hurt me. And yet, he wasn't, and in the meantime, I could focus on the tasty feeling that was having Patrick's cock in my mouth.

This was a lot messier than I thought it was going to be.

As that happened, Patrick appeared to be ready to shoot his come in my mouth, but it wasn't where he wanted it to go, so I wasn't surprised when he yanked his dick out of my mouth and pulled me to him hard, shoving it inside my pussy instead.

It was absolutely intoxicating the way he just stretched me. He went all the way inside of me, his balls the only thing that he could see. Then, I could feel his prick shooting his come in there, one hot rope after the other, and I knew that he was knocking me up.

I couldn't help but imagine how great it was going to be to have his heir in there.

Then, it was Charles' turn. He took me to him, made me go on all fours, and positioned himself inside of me, pistoning in and out of me with vigor and gusto. Moments later, I felt his come filling me up, and I couldn't contain my overflowing orgasm any longer.

It showered me with it, making my body writhe and convulse while Charles held me close to him. I couldn't read his mind, but it was more than obvious that he didn't want to pull out of my begging cunt even after cumming in me.

His fingers were digging into my skin as he then finally did that, and he was as sweaty as I was. In the meantime, I was panting as I looked at the ceiling and the light bulb hanging above my head. I just had one of the most amazing moments of my life and I would never forget it.

And I thought that Charles and Patrick were going to be jerks and leave me alone in the basement, but they actually stayed with me, each of them suckling and sucking on my boobs, draining every last drop of my milk.

This was a mouthwatering experience that would remain forever lodged in my mind.

EPILOGUE

I was looking at the ceiling and remembering how everything happened. I never thought that I would come here to get pregnant, but here I was, sitting on the patio, and my belly was full and heavy. My hands moved around it carefully and slowly, remembering that the doctors told me I was going to have duplets.

I couldn't help but feel excited about that.

And, by my side was Mary, who had her babies in her arms. She had triplets, something no one expected - not until they found out about it during one of their exams.

"They are so beautiful," I said, brushing my finger on the forehead of one of the babies.

"I'm glad you liked them. I'm so happy that I'm finally a mother," she said, smiling softly.

"I'm sure you're going to be a great mother," I said when I felt a pair of arms surrounding me and then pulling me up from where I was sitting. I was sitting on this short wall that surrounded the patio.

I snapped my head behind my shoulder and I found none other than Charles. His arms were around me and pressing against my body, but without hurting me.

I could feel his strong muscles against my skin, and he was making me feel so warm and safe that I couldn't imagine myself anywhere else right now.

"How are you feeling?" He asked, kissing the side of my neck as if he was my lover and we were actually in love, but that wasn't the case.

"Better than never," I responded, and then I turned around in his arms when he gave me enough space to do that.

I was naked, as I always was here in the Hucow Prison. Charles was a lawyer but he didn't look like one right now. If anything, he looked more like a bodybuilder that was visiting the prison.

I put my hand on his right pec, sliding it down before finding his junk. He was already hard, something I noticed when he had pressed his cock to my ass. Just remembering that, I was already missing it.

His eyes checked me from top to bottom, and I could see the lust that was in them. "Good Lord, you are so stunning," he cooed, settling his hands on my shoulders and then moving them down slowly and carefully, feeling every curve and part of me as if it was the first time he was doing this.

Then, I felt his hands massaging my belly as if he was showing me that being a father was something he wanted. I didn't know if that was the case for sure, but there was a good chance I was right.

I wrapped my fingers around his cock and started to stroke it gently and slowly, making it even harder than it was. He closed his eyes partially and looked at me with more lust than before.

"Jesus, are you really going to make me come right now?" He asked as he murmured, his fingers now playing with one of my nipples. "We are on the patio and everyone would see us doing it."

I moved in closer until I was feeling his hot breath against my face. Something was different about it, and it was much more than the minty hint that came with it.

"I don't think anybody would care – not even the guards," I murmured and he pulled up the right side of his lips slightly.

"You are so naughty that maybe I should punish you right now," he murmured, his fingers now pinching my nipple and shooting a wave of pleasure in my body. It made my nipple harder than it already was, and I just wanted him inside of me now more than ever.

"Maybe you should," I purred and then I got down on my knees even though it was difficult thanks to the extra weight in my body.

But I still managed to, and now my eyes were level with his cock. It was pointing at me, and seeing it so close to me was making me salivate as my lips went dry.

"Jesus, it's so meaty and juicy," I purred before putting my lips around his cock and beginning to bob up and down on it eagerly, covering it with my saliva, my pace frenetic from the get-go.

Seconds later, I realized that someone was by my side and that there was this sound of skin rubbing on skin coming from the same direction.

I reopened my eyes and snapped them to where the noise was coming from, finding none other than Patrick, who was glaring at me with threatening eyes.

"I don't know what you're thinking you're doing, princess, but you just can't have so much fun like this without me," he stated and then started to rub his hand on his dick faster, eventually going to the point where he was shooting his come all over me.

It was hot, creamy, and sticky. But if he thought he was punishing me by doing that, then he was going to be disappointed. What he just did, coming all over me, was enough to make me reach my climax as well.

And that happened at the same time as Charles started to unload his come inside my mouth, gracing me with his taste. In the meantime, Mary and everyone else were watching this with utmost attention, enjoying every second of it.

I pulled my head back and then started to clean up their cocks slowly and sexually, making sure I did that with my eyes locked on theirs.

I just never thought that serving my sentence at the Hucow Prison was going to be so satisfying. I was so glad that Charles made me come here.

The End

Thank you for reading this story, and leave your review. Your feedback helps me immensely!

TEASER: PASSED AROUND AT THE HUCOW PRISON

Steamy Milking Story

It was done. I did it. I was running from the police and they were coming after me as quickly as they could. Sweat was pooling on my forehead and in my armpits. It was difficult to be doing this. I was huffing, but I had a smile on my face.

I was certain that after they apprehended me, they were going to give me the sentence. I had no idea how many years I was going to have to spend in prison, but that wasn't an issue right now.

The issue was that I wanted them to give me another option – that of being sent to the Hucow Prison. My whole life, I'd been so ashamed of my body.

It was just incredibly skinny. Even my friends and other people that I held most dear to me, always mocked me about it. They always said that I was so skinny that no man would ever want me.

And considering that I was already 19 and was still a virgin, that appeared to be the case. I tried so many times to load up Tinder and find someone suitable to be my boyfriend, but it was impossible.

On Tinder, I always kept only photos of my face. At least,

according to many of the guys I talked to, they always said that I had a pretty face. It was what drew them to me, after all.

The problem came when they asked for photos of my body. It was then that they realized I was too skinny and that my breasts were too small. And from then, they always came up with excuses, saying that they weren't going to meet up with me in person because they were going to be busy with something else.

It was bullshit.

It was always bullshit and something that still hurt me so much.

It was with that thought in mind that I turned around quickly at a corner, proceeding down the alleyway between the buildings. Except for my tiny tank top and skirt that was so small it kept most of my legs exposed, I was almost naked.

Not to mention that my tank top kept my belly exposed, the air around me feeling a little too cold. It was supposed to be cold, though.

The stars were twinkling in the sky and the moon was high above the buildings. It was nighttime. One of the reasons why I liked to wear skimpy clothes was because I wanted to feel better about myself. I wanted people to know that there was at least something else other than my face that could make men lust after me, even though that wasn't working well.

I wanted men to notice how smooth my skin was without touching it. Even though it was dark, it shone under the light coming from a nearby light pole. It was a momentary thing, but I glanced down to look at the shine on my skin when the light brushed over it.

I also wore a pair of small shoes that didn't make me taller than I was. To be honest, I was small and didn't mind that. I could make myself taller with a pair of heeled sandals or boots, but it would serve me no purpose.

Since I was skinny and my breasts were tiny, I had to compensate by doing those things. Wearing skimpy clothes, small shoes that didn't make me taller, skin cream to make my body even more relucent under any light conditions, and using some of the best perfumes in the world.

It couldn't be any different. But this was also a different world, a world where most men favored women with big jugs where they could bury their faces into, and I just wasn't a good fit for that. I couldn't do anything to change that, too, I thought as I turned at another corner.

I was running from the police as fast as I could so that they didn't suspect something was up. My hand was holding a small collection of jewels. They were some of the most expensive in the city. The store's owner was someone I knew well and I also knew a couple of things about the building which allowed me to sneak in there easily.

And after that, it was easy for me to get my hands on this small box. I was clutching it tightly. This would all go downhill if I dropped it and I couldn't let that happen.

And I was just about to turn around another corner when something heavy and hard hit me on my face, making me fall over heavily on the ground. Looking up, I realized that it was one of the policemen that were chasing me. I knew those police officers in this town were rough and cruel, but I never thought they were just going to hit me in the face like this.

I stood up slowly and then police officers came from behind me quickly, snapping handcuffs on my wrists. It happened so quickly that I wasn't able to do anything about it. One moment I was with my arms free, and the next the handcuffs were on my wrists.

"We got you now, you little thief," the officer that was in front of me happily said as he approached me.

I smiled. There was no point in denying that this was the outcome I wanted. There was going to be a round of questions, but I was going to be ready for them. Not to mention that I could barely wait for that.

The officers were going to present me with two options. Either I could serve my sentence at a normal jail or I could go to the hucow prison, where I actually wanted to go.

Finally, my body was going to become curvy and busty.

The officer's eyes looked me up and down as if he was finding my frame pathetic.

And a moment later, he said, "Well, little miss, we have no idea why you were stealing this box of jewels, but your time has run out. You are coming with us now."

SIMILAR BOOKS

SERIES - FAVORITE HUCOWS

1. First Time in the Barn

2. First Time in the Pen

3. First Time in the Shed

4. First Time in the Tractor

5. First Time on the Haystack

SERIES - FERTILE ONLY

1. Bumping the Teacher

2. Bumping the Midwife

3. Bumping the Farmhand

4. Bumping the Sinner

ABOUT THE AUTHOR

Leandra Camilli's obsession? Writing dirty, steamy stories that make her readers drool. She loves her Alpha males, hucows, sissies, and futas. If you're looking for those kinds of books, look no further.

With a cup of coffee on her table and warm socks on, she writes almost every day. Leandra Camilli has featured in several top 100 categories in the store, and she publishes weekly.